My Day in the Garden

WRITTEN & ILLUSTRATED BY

Carolyn Seabolt

ISBN: 978-1-60414-929-6

For information, please contact
Fideli Publishing, Inc.:
info@fidelipublishing.com
www.FideliPublishing.com

My name is Roxanne,

Roxy for short.

I'm a seal point Siamese.

I have beautiful blue eyes, and

dark brown stockings and tail.

I'm fairly quiet for a Siamese cat,

but I do enjoy purring.

I live at Cat Tracks Studio

in a small rural town in Maryland.

My owner (I just let her think that)

is an artist and a gardener,

so I have a great place

to call my own.

My human is up early in the morning.

After a quick breakfast,

we are out the door

and into the garden,

while the temperature

is cool.

As we walk together,

we enjoy the flowers

and listening to the

early morning quiet.

We carry water
from the
rain barrel
to give
the flowers
a drink.
We also fill
the bird baths
with clean
fresh water.

I like to sit

and watch

my bird friends

as they splash

in the water.

They are so silly.

They think I want

to get wet too!

We have lots
of human visitors
at the studio
and garden.
We also have
my friends rabbit and mouse,
and lots of birds,
and beautiful butterflies
in the summer.

Sometimes I get to invite
a few of my
feline friends over to play.
We love to chase
each other around the trees
and sometimes I even
run up a tree!
What a great view
from up high.
In the spring, I often see
a bird nest with eggs
waiting to hatch.

I like to hide
in the flowers
waiting for
something to move
so I can
jump at it.
Usually it's just
my brother Oliver
looking for me.
He always thinks
I'm lost.

In the late morning
the sun warms
my back and a cool
summer breeze
blows through
my whiskers.
It's time for a nap,
so I find
just the perfect
place.

In the afternoon
when my nap is through,
it's time for more adventures.
I love to explore deep inside the flowers
I walked by in the morning.
There I find Lilly the lady bug,
Greg the garden spider
working on his web, and
caterpillars munching away.
Sometimes I even find
my toad friend, Fred.

It's really fun in here!

My human
sometimes
calls me
a princess.
I like that.
I think I look lovely
with my crown
and flowers
in my fur.

As I make my way
up the steps
to the upper garden,
I stop to play
in the sunflowers
and watch the
butterflies flutter by.
Sometimes they
get so close,
my eyes cross
as I watch them.

We grow all kinds
of vegetables in the garden:
corn, red beets, tomatoes
and cabbage to mention
just a few.
I like to walk through them
and look at all the colors.
The most fun, though, is
getting a ride in the
wheelbarrow.

In Autumn,

when the pumpkins

turn orange and

the leaves begin to fall,

it's fun to hide

in the piles of leaves

my human rakes up.

I jump out and scare her,

and after a chase,

I fall down

to get a belly rub.

It's my

favorite thing!

As the sun begins
to set in the garden,
we walk back
to the studio, this time
listening to the sounds
of the evening.
I had lots of adventures
today, and I will
dream of them tonight.

Life is good!

About the Author

I have always wanted to write and illustrate children's books.

After many years of illustrating for other writers, this is my first book written and illustrated by me.

My studio is called Cat Tracks. I am pleased to share it with my two beautiful Siamese cats named Oliver and Roxanne.

The studio is surrounded by many gardens, which are a constant source of inspirations for my artwork.

I am a graduate of the Maryland Institute College of Art in Baltimore, Maryland, with at BFA/MFA in art education.

CPSIA information can be obtained
at www.ICGtesting.com
Printed in the USA
BVOW07*0640060916

R7392300001B/R73923PG460886BVX1B/1/P